Funnyhouse of

A Negro

A PLAY IN ONE ACT

By Adrienne Kennedy

SAMUEL FRENCH, INC.

25 WEST 45TH STREET   NEW YORK 10036
7623 SUNSET BOULEVARD   HOLLYWOOD 90046
LONDON   *TORONTO*

CHARACTERS

NEGRO-SARAH

DUCHESS OF HAPSBURG .... *One of herselves*

QUEEN VICTORIA REGINA .... *One of herselves*

JESUS .... *One of herselves*

PATRICE LUMUMBA .... *One of herselves*

SARAH'S LANDLADY .... *Funnyhouse Lady*

RAYMOND .... *Funnyhouse Man*

THE MOTHER

AUTHOR'S NOTE

FUNNYHOUSE OF A NEGRO is perhaps clearest and most explicit when the play is placed in the girl Sarah's room. The center of the stage works well as her room, allowing the rest of the stage as the place for herselves. Her room should have a bed, a writing table and a mirror. Near her bed is the statue of Queen Victoria; other objects might be her photographs and her books. When she is placed in her room with her belongings, then the director is free to let the rest of the play happen around her.

Funnyhouse of A Negro

BEGINNING: *Before the closed Curtain* A WOMAN *dressed in a white nightgown walks across the Stage carrying before her a bald head. She moves as one in a trance and is mumbling something inaudible to herself. Her hair is wild, straight and black and falls to her waist. As she moves, she gives the effect of one in a dream. She crosses the Stage from Right to Left. Before she has barely vanished, the CURTAIN opens. It is a white satin Curtain of a cheap material and a ghastly white, a material that brings to mind the interior of a cheap casket, parts of it are frayed and look as if it has been gnawed by rats.*

THE SCENE: TWO WOMEN *are sitting in what appears to be a Queen's chamber. It is set in the middle of the Stage in a strong white LIGHT, while the rest of the Stage is in unnatural BLACKNESS. The quality of the white light is unreal and ugly. The Queen's chamber consists of a dark monumental bed resembling an ebony tomb, a low, dark chandelier with candles, and wine-colored walls. Flying about are great black RAVENS.* QUEEN VICTORIA *is standing before her bed holding a small mirror in her hand. On the white pillow of her bed is a dark, indistinguishable object.* THE DUCHESS OF HAPSBURG *is standing at the foot of the bed. Her back is to us as is the* QUEEN'S. *Throughout the entire scene, they do not move.* BOTH WOMEN *are dressed in royal gowns of white, a white similar to the white of the Curtain,*

*the material cheap satin. Their headpieces are white
and of a net that falls over their faces. From beneath
both their headpieces springs a headful of wild kinky
hair. Although in this scene we do not see their faces,
I will describe them now. They look exactly alike and
will wear masks or be made up to appear a whitish
yellow. It is an alabaster face, the skin drawn tightly
over the high cheekbones, great dark eyes that seem
gouged out of the head, a high forehead, a full red
mouth and a head of frizzy hair. If the characters do
not wear a mask then the face must be highly pow-
dered and possess a hard expressionless quality and
a stillness as in the face of death. We hear KNOCK-
ING.*

VICTORIA. (*Listening to the knocking.*) It is my father.
He is arriving again for the night. (*The* DUCHESS *makes
no reply.*) He comes through the jungle to find me. He
never tires of his journey.

DUCHESS. How dare he enter the castle, he who is the
darkest of them all, the darkest one? My mother looked
like a white woman, hair as straight as any white
woman's. And at least I am yellow, but he is black, the
blackest one of them all. I hoped he was dead. Yet he
still comes through the jungle to find me.

(*The KNOCKING is louder.*)

VICTORIA. He never tires of the journey, does he,
Duchess? (*Looking at herself in the mirror.*)

DUCHESS. How dare he enter the castle of Queen Victoria Regina, Monarch of England? It is because of him
that my mother died. The wild black beast put his hands
on her. She died.

VICTORIA. Why does he keep returning? He keeps returning forever, coming back ever and keeps coming back
forever. He is my father.

DUCHESS. He is a black Negro.

VICTORIA. He is my father. I am tied to the black Negro. He came when I was a child in the south, before I was born he haunted my conception, diseased my birth.

DUCHESS. Killed my mother.

VICTORIA. My mother was the light. She was the lightest one. She looked like a white woman.

DUCHESS. We are tied to him unless, of course, he should die.

VICTORIA. But he is dead.

DUCHESS. And he keeps returning.

(*The KNOCKING is louder; BLACKOUT. The LIGHTS go out in the Chamber. Onto the Stage from the Left comes the* FIGURE *in the white nightgown carrying the bald head. This time we hear her speak.*)

MOTHER. Black man, black man, I never should have let a black man put his hands on me. The wild black beast raped me and now my skull is shining. (*She disappears to the Right.*)

(*Now the LIGHT is focused on a single white square wall that is to the Left of the Stage, that is suspended and stands alone, of about five feet in dimension and width. It stands with the narrow part facing the audience. A* CHARACTER *steps through. She is a faceless, dark character with a hangman's rope about her neck and red blood on the part that would be her face. She is the* NEGRO. *The most noticeable aspect of her looks is her wild kinky hair. It is a ragged head with a patch of hair missing from the crown which the* NEGRO *carries in her hand. She is dressed in black. She steps slowly through the wall, stands still before it and begins her monologue:*)

NEGRO. Part of the time I live with Raymond, part of

the time with God, Maxmilliam and Albert Saxe Coburg. I live in my room. It is a small room on the top floor of a brownstone in the West Nineties in New York, a room filled with my dark old volumes, a narrow bed and on the wall old photographs of castles and monarchs of England. It is also Victoria's chamber. Queen Victoria Regina's. Partly because it is consumed by a gigantic plaster statue of Queen Victoria who is my idol and partly for other reasons; three steps that I contrived out of boards lead to the statue which I have placed opposite the door as I enter the room. It is a sitting figure, a replica of one in London, and a thing of astonishing whiteness. I found it in a dusty shop on Morningside Heights. Raymond says it is a thing of terror, possessing the quality of nightmares, suggesting large and probable deaths. And of course he is right. When I am the Duchess of Hapsburg I sit opposite Victoria in my headpiece and we talk. The other time I wear the dress of a student, dark clothes and dark stockings. Victoria always wants me to tell her of whiteness. She wants me to tell her of a royal world where everything and everyone is white and there are no unfortunate black ones. For as we of royal blood know, black is evil and has been from the beginning. Even before my mother's hair started to fall out. Before she was raped by a wild black beast. Black was evil.

As for myself I long to become even a more pallid Negro than I am now; pallid like Negroes on the covers of American Negro magazines; soulless, educated and irreligious. I want to possess no moral value, particularly value as to my being. I want not to be. I ask nothing except anonymity. I am an English major, as my mother was when she went to school in Atlanta. My father majored in Social Work. I am graduated from a city college and have occasional work in libraries, but mostly spend my days preoccupied with the placement and geometric position of words on paper. I write poetry filling white page after white page with imitations of Edith Sitwell. It is my dream to live in rooms with European antiques and my Queen Victoria, photographs of Roman ruins, walls of books, a piano, oriental carpets and to eat my meals on a white glass table. I will visit my friends' apartments which will contain books, photographs of Roman ruins, pianos and oriental carpets. My friends will be white.

I need them as an embankment to keep me from reflecting too much upon the fact that I am a Negro. For, like all educated Negroes—out of life and death essential—I find it necessary to maintain a stark fortress against recognition of myself. My white friends, like myself, will be shrewd, intellectual and anxious for death. Anyone's death. I will mistrust them, as I do myself, waver in their opinion of me, as I waver in the opinion of myself. But if I had not wavered in my opinion of myself, then my hair would never have fallen out. And if my hair hadn't fallen out, I wouldn't have bludgeoned my father's head with an ebony mask.

In appearance I am good-looking in a boring way; no glaring Negroid features, medium nose, medium mouth and pale yellow skin. My one defect is that I have a head of frizzy hair, unmistakably Negro kinky hair; and it is indistinguishable. I would like to lie and say I love Raymond. But I do not. He is a poet and is Jewish. He is very interested in Negroes.

(*The* NEGRO *stands by the wall and throughout her following speech, the following characters come through the wall, disappearing off into varying directions in the darkened night of the Stage:* DUCHESS, QUEEN VICTORIA, JESUS, PATRICE LUMUMBA. JESUS *is a hunchback, yellow-skinned dwarf, dressed in white rags and sandals.* PATRICE LUMUMBA *is a black man. His head appears to be split in two with blood and tissue in eyes. He carries an ebony mask.*)

SARAH'S (NEGRO) SECOND SPEECH. The rooms are my rooms; a Hapsburg chamber, a chamber in a Victorian castle, the hotel where I killed my father, the jungle. These are the places myselves exist in. I know no places. That is, I cannot believe in places. To believe in places is to know hope and to know the emotion of hope is to know beauty. It links us across a horizon and connects us to the world. I find there are no places only my funnyhouse. Streets are rooms, cities are rooms, eternal rooms. I try to create a space for myselves in cities, New York, the midwest, a southern town, but it becomes a lie. I try to give myselves a logical relationship but that too is a lie. For relationships was one of my last religions. I clung loyally to the lie of relationships, again and again seeking to establish a connection between my characters. Jesus is Victoria's son. Mother loved my father before her hair fell out. A loving relationship exists between myself and Queen Victoria, a love between myself and Jesus but they are lies.

(*Then to the Right front of the Stage comes the WHITE LIGHT. It goes to a suspended stairway. At the foot of it, stands the* LANDLADY. *She is a tall, thin, white woman dressed in a black and red hat and appears to be talking to someone in a suggested open doorway in a corridor of a rooming house. She laughs like a mad character in a funnyhouse throughout her speech.*)

LANDLADY. (*Who is looking up the stairway.*) Ever since her father hung himself in a Harlem hotel when Patrice Lumumba was murdered she hides herself in her room. Each night she repeats: He keeps returning. How dare he enter the castle walls, he who is the darkest of them all, the darkest one? My mother looked like a white woman, hair as straight as any white woman's. And I am yellow but he, he is black, the blackest one of them all. I hoped he was dead. Yet he still comes through the jungle.

I tell her: Sarah, honey, the man hung himself. It's not

your blame. But, no, she stares at me: No, Mrs. Conrad, he did not hang himself, that is only the way they understand it, they do, but the truth is that I bludgeoned his head with an ebony skull that he carries about with him. Wherever he goes, he carries black masks and heads.

She's suffering so till her hair has fallen out. But then she did always hide herself in that room with the walls of books and her statue. I always did know she thought she was somebody else, a Queen or something, somebody else.

BLACKOUT

SCENE: *Funnyman's place.*

The next scene is enacted with the DUCHESS and RAYMOND. Raymond's place is suggested as being above the Negro's room and is etched in with a prop of blinds and a bed. Behind the blinds are mirrors and when the blinds are opened and closed by Raymond this is revealed. RAYMOND turns out to be the funnyman of the funnyhouse. He is tall, white and ghostly thin and dressed in a black shirt and black trousers in attire suggesting an artist. Throughout his dialogue he laughs. The DUCHESS is partially disrobed and it is implied from their attitudes of physical intimacy— he is standing and she is sitting before him clinging to his leg. During the scene RAYMOND keeps opening and closing the blinds.

DUCHESS. (*Carrying a red paper bag.*) My father is arriving and what am I to do?

(RAYMOND *walks about the place opening the blinds and laughing.*)

FUNNYMAN. He is arriving from Africa, is he not?

DUCHESS. Yes, yes, he is arriving from Africa.

FUNNYMAN. I always knew your father was African.

DUCHESS. He is an African who lives in the jungle. He is an African who has always lived in the jungle. Yes, he is a nigger who is an African who is a missionary teacher and is now dedicating his life to the erection of a Christian mission in the middle of the jungle. He is a black man.

FUNNYMAN. He is a black man who shot himself when they murdered Patrice Lumumba.

DUCHESS. (*Goes on wildly.*) Yes, my father is a black man who went to Africa years ago as a missionary teacher, got mixed up in politics, was revealed and is now devoting his foolish life to the erection of a Christian mission in the middle of the jungle in one of those newly freed countries. Hide me. (*Clinging to his knees.*) Hide me here so the nigger will not find me.

FUNNYMAN. (*Laughing.*) Your father is in the jungle dedicating his life to the erection of a Christian mission.

DUCHESS. Hide me here so the jungle will not find me. Hide me.

FUNNYMAN. Isn't it cruel of you?

DUCHESS. Hide me from the jungle.

FUNNYMAN. Isn't it cruel?

DUCHESS. No, no.

FUNNYMAN. Isn't it cruel of you?

DUCHESS. No. (*She screams and opens her red paper bag and draws from it her fallen hair. It is a great mass of dark wild. She holds it up to him. He appears not to understand. He stares at it.*) It is my hair. (*He continues to stare at her.*) When I awakened this morning it had fallen out, not all of it but a mass from the crown of my head that lay on the center of my pillow. I arose and in the greyish winter morning light of my room I stood staring at my hair, dazed by my sleeplessness, still shaken by nightmares of my mother. Was it true, yes, it was my hair. In the mirror I saw that, although my hair remained on both sides, clearly on the crown and at my temples my scalp was bare. (*She removes her black crown and shows him the top of her head.*)

FUNNYMAN. (*Staring at her.*) Why would your hair fall out? Is it because you are cruel? How could a black father haunt you so?

DUCHESS. He haunted my very conception. He was a wild black beast who raped my mother.

FUNNYMAN. He is a black Negro. (*Laughing.*)

DUCHESS. Ever since I can remember he's been in a nigger pose of agony. He is the wilderness. He speaks niggerly groveling about wanting to touch me with his black hand.

FUNNYMAN. How tormented and cruel you are.

DUCHESS. (*As if not comprehending.*) Yes, yes, the man's dark, very dark-skinned. He is the darkest, my father is the darkest, my mother is the lightest. I am in between. But my father is the darkest. My father is a nigger who drives me to misery. Any time spent with him evolves itself into suffering. He is a black man and the wilderness.

FUNNYMAN. How tormented and cruel you are.

DUCHESS. He is a nigger.

FUNNYMAN. And your mother, where is she?

DUCHESS. She is in the asylum. In the asylum bald. Her father was a white man. And she is in the asylum.

(*He takes her in his arms. She responds wildly.*)

BLACKOUT

KNOCKING is heard; it continues, then somewhere near the Center of the Stage a FIGURE appears in the darkness, a large dark faceless MAN carrying a mask in his hand.

MAN. It begins with the disaster of my hair. I awaken. My hair has fallen out, not all of it, but a mass from the crown of my head that lies on the center of my white pillow. I arise and in the greyish winter morning light of my room I stand staring at my hair, dazed by sleeplessness, still shaken by nightmares of my mother. Is it true? Yes. It is my hair. In the mirror I see that although my hair remains on both sides, clearly on the crown and at my temples my scalp is bare. And in the sleep I had been visited by my bald crazy mother who comes to me crying, calling me to her bedside. She lies on the bed watching the strands of her own hair fall out. Her hair fell out after she married and she spent her days lying on the bed watching the strands fall from her scalp, covering the bedspread until she was bald and admitted to the hospital. Black man, black man, my mother says, I never should have let a black man put his hands on me. She comes to me, her bald skull shining. Black diseases, Sarah, she says. Black diseases. I run. She follows me, her bald skull shining. That is the beginning.

    heads.)

BLACKOUT

SCENE: *Queen's Chamber.*

Her hair is in a small pile on the bed and in a small pile on the floor, several other small piles of hair are scattered about her and her white gown is covered with fallen out hair. QUEEN VICTORIA *acts out the following scene: She awakens (in pantomime) and discovers her hair has fallen. It is on her pillow. She arises and stands at the side of the bed with her back toward us, staring at hair. The* DUCHESS *enters the room, comes around, standing behind* VICTORIA, *and they stare at the hair.* VICTORIA *picks up a mirror. The* DUCHESS *then picks up a mirror and looks at her own hair. She opens the red paper bag that she is carrying and takes out her hair, attempting to place it back on her head (for unlike* VICTORIA, *she does not wear her headpiece now). The LIGHTS remain on. The unidentified* MAN *returns out of the darkness and speaks. He carries the mask.*

MAN. (*Patrice Lumumba.*) I am a nigger of two generations. I am Patrice Lumumba. I am a nigger of two generations. I am the black shadow that haunted my mother's conception. I belong to the generation born at the turn of the century and the generation born before the depression. At present I reside in New York City in a brownstone in the West Nineties. I am an English major at a city college. My nigger father majored in social work, so did my mother. I am a student and have occasional work in libraries. But mostly I spend my vile days preoccupied with the placement and geometric position of words on paper. I write poetry filling white page after white page with imitations of Sitwell. It is my vile dream to live in rooms with European antiques and my statue of Queen Victoria, photographs of Roman ruins, walls of books, a piano and oriental carpets and to eat my meals on a white glass table. It is also my nigger dream for my friends to eat their meals on white glass tables and to live in rooms with European antiques, photographs of Roman ruins, pianos and oriental carpets. My friends will be white. I need them as an embankment to keep me from reflecting too much upon the fact that I am Patrice Lumumba who haunted my mother's conception. They are necessary for me to maintain recognition against myself. My white friends, like myself, will be shrewd intellectuals and anxious for death. Anyone's death. I will despise them as I do myself. For if I did not despise myself then my hair would not have fallen and if my hair had not fallen then I would not have bludgeoned my father's face with the ebony mask.

(*The LIGHT remains on him. Before him a BALD HEAD is dropped on a wire,* SOMEONE *screams. An-*

*other wall is dropped, larger than the first one was.
This one is near the front of the Stage facing thus.
Throughout the following monologue, the* CHAR-
ACTERS: DUCHESS, VICTORIA, JESUS *go back and
forth. As they go in their backs are to us but the*
NEGRO *faces us, speaking:*)

I always dreamed of a day when my mother would smile
at me. My father . . . his mother wanted him to be
Christ. From the beginning in the lamp of their dark room
she said—I want you to be Jesus, to walk in Genesis and
save the race. You must return to Africa, find revelation
in the midst of golden savannas, nim and white frankopenny trees, white stallions roaming under a blue sky, you
must walk with a white dove and heal the race, heal the
misery, take us off the cross. She stared at him anguished
in the kerosene light . . . At dawn he watched her rise,
kill a hen for him to eat at breakfast, then go to work
down at the big house till dusk, till she died.

His father told him the race was no damn good. He
hated his father and adored his mother. His mother didn't
want him to marry my mother and sent a dead chicken to
the wedding. I DON'T want you marrying that child, she
wrote, she's not good enough for you, I want you to go to
Africa. When they first married they lived in New York.
Then they went to Africa where my mother fell out of
love with my father. She didn't want him to save the
black race and spent her days combing her hair. She would
not let him touch her in their wedding bed and called him
black. He is black of skin with dark eyes and a great
dark square brow. Then in Africa he started to drink and
came home drunk one night and raped my mother. The
child from the union is me. I clung to my mother. Long
after she went to the asylum I wove dreams of her
beauty, her straight hair and fair skin and grey eyes, so
identical to mine. How it anguished him. I turned from
him, nailing him on the cross, he said, dragging him

through grass and nailing him on a cross until he bled. He pleaded with me to help him find Genesis, search for Genesis in the midst of golden savannas, nim and white frankopenny trees and white stallions roaming under a blue sky, help him search for the white doves, he wanted the black man to make a pure statement, he wanted the black man to rise from colonialism. But I sat in the room with my mother, sat by her bedside and helped her comb her straight black hair and wove long dreams of her beauty. She had long since begun to curse the place and spoke of herself trapped in blackness. She preferred the company of night owls. Only at night did she rise, walking in the garden among the trees with the owls. When I spoke to her she saw I was a black man's child and she preferred speaking to owls. Nights my father came from his school in the village struggling to embrace me. But I fled and hid under my mother's bed while she screamed of remorse. Her hair was falling badly and after a while we had to return to this country.

He tried to hang himself once. After my mother went to the asylum he had hallucinations, his mother threw a dead chicken at him, his father laughed and said the race was no damn good, my mother appeared in her nightgown screaming she had trapped herself in blackness. No white doves flew. He had left Africa and was again in New York. He lived in Harlem and no white doves flew. Sarah, Sarah, he would say to me, the soldiers are coming and a cross they are placing high on a tree and are dragging me through the grass and nailing me upon the cross. My blood is gushing. I wanted to live in Genesis in the midst of golden savannas, nim and white frankopenny trees and white stallions roaming under a blue sky. I wanted to walk with a white dove. I wanted to be a Christian. Now I am Judas. I betrayed my mother. I sent your mother to the asylum. I created a yellow child who hates me. And he tried to hang himself in a Harlem hotel.

BLACKOUT

(*A BALD HEAD is dropped on a string. We hear LAUGHING.*)

SCENE: *Duchess's place.*

The next scene is done in the Duchess of Hapsburg's place which is a chandeliered ballroom with SNOW falling, a black and white marble floor, a bench decorated with white flowers, all of this can be made of obviously fake materials as they would be in a funnyhouse. The DUCHESS *is wearing a white dress and as in the previous scene a white headpiece with her kinky hair springing out from under it. In the scene are the* DUCHESS *and* JESUS. JESUS *enters the room, which is at first dark, then suddenly BRILLIANT, he starts to cry out at the* DUCHESS, *who is seated on a bench under the chandelier, and pulls his hair from the red paper bag holding it up for the* DUCHESS *to see.*

JESUS. My hair. (*The* DUCHESS *does not speak,* JESUS *again screams.*) My hair. (*Holding the hair up, waiting for a reaction from the* DUCHESS.)

DUCHESS. (*As if oblivious.*) I have something I must show you. (*She goes quickly to shutters and darkens the room, returning standing before* JESUS. *She then slowly removes her headpiece and from under it takes a mass of her hair.*) When I awakened I found it fallen out, not all of it but a mass that lay on my white pillow. I could see, although my hair hung down at the sides, clearly on my white scalp it was missing.

(*Her baldness is identical to* JESUS's.)

BLACKOUT

The LIGHTS come back up. They are BOTH *sitting on the bench examining each other's hair, running it through their fingers, then slowly the* DUCHESS *disappears behind the shutters and returns with a long red comb. She sits on the bench next to* JESUS *and starts to comb her remaining hair over her baldness. (This is done slowly.)* JESUS *then takes the comb and proceeds to do the same to the* DUCHESS *of Hapsburg's hair. After they finish they place the* DUCHESS'S *headpiece back on and we can see the strands of their hair falling to the floor.* JESUS *then lies down across the bench while the* DUCHESS *walks back and forth, the KNOCKING does not cease. They speak in unison as the* DUCHESS *walks about and* JESUS *lies on the bench in the falling snow, staring at the ceiling.*

DUCHESS and JESUS. *(Their hair is falling more now, they are both hideous.)* My father isn't going to let us alone. *(KNOCKING.)* Our father isn't going to let us alone, our father is the darkest of us all, my mother was the fairest, I am in between, but my father is the darkest of them all. He is a black man. Our father is the darkest of them all. He is a black man. My father is a dead man.

(Then they suddenly look up at each other and scream, the LIGHTS go to their heads and we see that they are totally bald. There is a KNOCKING. LIGHTS go to the stairs and the LANDLADY.*)*

LANDLADY. He wrote to her saying he loved her and asked her forgiveness. He begged her to take him off the cross, *(He had dreamed she would.)* stop them from tormenting him, the one with the chicken and his cursing father. Her mother's hair fell out, the race's hair fell out because he left Africa, he said. He had tried to save them. She must embrace him. He said his existence depended on

her embrace. He wrote her from Africa where he is creating
his Christian center in the jungle and that is why he came
here. I know that he wanted her to return there with him
and not desert the race. He came to see her once before he
tried to hang himself, appearing in the corridor of my
apartment. I had let him in. I found him sitting on a
bench in the hallway. He put out his hand to her, tried to
take her in his arms, crying out—Forgiveness, Sarah, is
it that you never will forgive me for being black? Sarah,
I know you were a child of torment. But forgiveness. That
was before his breakdown. Then, he wrote her and repeated that his mother hoped he would be Christ but he
failed. He had married her mother because he .could not
resist the light. Yet, his mother from the beginning in the
kerosene lamp of their dark rooms in Georgia said: I want
you to be Jesus, to walk in Genesis and save the race, return to Africa, find revelation in the black. He went away.

But Easter morning, she got to feeling badly and went
into Harlem to see him; the streets were filled with
vendors selling lilacs. He had checked out of that hotel.
When she arrived back at my brownstone he was here,
dressed badly, rather drunk, I had let him in again. He
sat on a bench in the dark hallway, put out his hand to
her, trying to take her in his arms, crying out—forgiveness, Sarah, forgiveness for my being black, Sarah. I know
you are a child of torment. I know on dark winter after-
noons you sit alone weaving stories of your mother's
beauty. But Sarah, answer me, don't turn away, Sarah.
Forgive my blackness. She would not answer. He put out his
hand to her. She ran past him on the stairs, left him there
with his hand out to me, repeating his past, saying his
mother hoped he would be Christ. From the beginning in
the kerosene lamp of their dark rooms, she said: "Wally,
I want you to be Jesus, to walk in Genesis and save the
race. You must return to Africa, Wally, find revelation in
the midst of golden savannas, nim and white frankopenny
trees and white stallions roaming under a blue sky. Wally,

you must find the white dove and heal the pain of the race, heal the misery of the black man, Wally, take us off the cross, Wally." In the kerosene light she stared at me anguished from her old Negro face—but she ran past him leaving him. And now he is dead, she says, now he is dead. He left Africa and now Patrice Lumumba is dead.

(*The next scene is enacted back in the* DUCHESS *of Hapsburg's place.* JESUS *is still in the Duchess's chamber, apparently he has fallen asleep and as we see him he awakens with the* DUCHESS *by his side, and sits here as in a trance. He rises terrified and speaks.*)

JESUS. Through my apocalypses and my raging sermons I have tried so to escape him, through God Almighty I have tried to escape being black. (*He then appears to rouse himself from his thoughts and calls:*) Duchess, Duchess. (*He looks about for her, there is no answer. He gets up slowly, walks back into the darkness and there we see that she is hanging on the chandelier, her bald head suddenly drops to the floor and she falls upon* JESUS. *He screams.*) I am going to Africa and kill this black man named Patrice Lumumba. Why? Because all my life I believed my Holy Father to be God, but now I know that my father is a black man. I have no fear for whatever I do, I will do in the name of God, I will do in the name of Albert Saxe Coburg, in the name of Victoria, Queen Victoria Regina, the monarch of England, I will.

BLACKOUT

SCENE: *In the jungle, RED SUN, FLYING THINGS, wild black grass. The effect of the jungle is that it, unlike the other Scenes, is over the entire Stage. In time this is the longest Scene in the play and is played the slowest, as the slow, almost standstill stages of a dream. By lighting the desired effect would be—suddenly the jungle has overgrown the chambers and all the other places with a violence and a dark brightness, a grim yellowness.*

JESUS *is the first to appear in the center of the jungle darkness. Unlike in previous scenes, he has a nimbus above his head. As they each successively appear, they all too have nimbuses atop their heads in a manner to suggest that they are saviours.*

JESUS. I always believed my father to be God.

(*Suddenly they all appear in various parts of the jungle.* PATRICE LUMUMBA, THE DUCHESS, VICTORIA, *wandering about speaking at once. Their speeches are mixed and repeated by one another:*)

ALL. He never tires of the journey, he who is the darkest one, the darkest one of them all. My mother looked like a white woman, hair as straight as any white woman's. I am yellow but he is black, the darkest one of us all. How I hoped he was dead, yet he never tires of the journey. It was because of him that my mother died because she let a black man put his hands on her. Why does he keep returning? He keeps returning forever, keeps returning and returning and he is my father. He is a black Negro. They told me my Father was God but my father is black. He is my father. I am tied to a black Negro. He returned when I lived in the south back in the twenties, when I was a child, he returned. Before I was born at the turn of the century, he haunted my conception, diseased my birth . . . killed my mother. He killed the light. My mother was the lightest one. I am bound to him unless, of course, he should die.
But he is dead.
And he keeps returning. Then he is not dead.
Then he is not dead.

Yet, he is dead, but dead he comes knocking at my door.

(This is repeated several times, finally reaching a loud pitch and then ALL *rushing about the grass. They stop and stand perfectly still.* ALL *speaking tensely at various times in a chant.)*

I see him. The black ugly thing is sitting in his hallway, surrounded by his ebony masks, surrounded by the blackness of himself. My mother comes into the room. He is there with his hand out to me, grovelling, saying—Forgiveness, Sarah, is it that you will never forgive me for being black.

Forgiveness, Sarah, I know you are a nigger of torment. Why? Christ would not rape anyone.

You will never forgive me for being black.

Wild beast. Why did you rape my mother? Black beast, Christ would not rape anyone.

He is in grief from that black anguished face of his. Then at once the room will grow bright and my mother will come toward me smiling while I stand before his face and bludgeon him with an ebony head.

Forgiveness, Sarah, I know you are a nigger of torment.

(Silence. Then they suddenly begin to laugh and shout as though they are in victory. They continue for some minutes running about laughing and shouting.)

BLACKOUT

Another WALL drops. There is a white plaster statue of Queen Victoria which represents the Negro's room in the brownstone, the room appears near the staircase highly lit and small. The main prop is the statue but a bed could be suggested. The figure of Victoria is a sitting figure, one of astonishing repulsive white-ness, suggested by dusty volumes of books and old yellowed walls.

The Negro SARAH *is standing perfectly still, we hear the KNOCKING, the LIGHTS come on quickly, her* FATHER'S *black figure with bludgeoned hands rushes upon her, the LIGHT GOES BLACK and we see her hanging in the room.*

LIGHTS come on the laughing LANDLADY. *And at the same time remain on the hanging figure of the* NEGRO.

LANDLADY. The poor bitch has hung herself. (FUNNY-MAN RAYMOND *appears from his room at the commotion.*) The poor bitch has hung herself.

RAYMOND. (*Observing her hanging figure.*) She was a funny little liar.

LANDLADY. (*Informing him.*) Her father hung himself in a Harlem hotel when Patrice Lumumba died.

RAYMOND. Her father never hung himself in a Harlem hotel when Patrice Lumumba was murdered. I know the man. He is a doctor, married to a white whore. He lives in the city in rooms with European antiques, photographs of Roman ruins, walls of books and oriental carpets. Her father is a nigger who eat his meals on a white glass table.

END

LADY KILLERS

Farce. 1 act. By John Kirkpatrick.

6 females. Interior. Modern costumes. 40 minutes.

Miriam's husband laughed at her when she made a speech at a college reunion. Edna, her spinster friend, advocated divorce. Lottie, who had left her husband, said the only effective way to get rid of a husband was to—well—eliminate him. Edna arranged with Bernice, who had disposed of at least two, to dispose of four more husbands—Caroline and Jenny had somehow got into it too. It was a wonderful scheme: The only trouble with it was it boomeranged.

(Royalty, $5.00.)

THE FIFTH WHEEL

Comedy. 1 act. By Marjean Perry.

5 females. Interior.

The scatterbrained Mrs. Hilda Finch, during the six months she has belonged to the Woman's Club, has managed to create a lot of turmoil by an excess of enthusiasm and imagination. Now she's planning a membership campaign to make up to everyone for past mistakes. The officers of the Club, horrified by her impractical plan, try to stop her before it's too late—with mixed success.

(Royalty, $5.00.)

WILL THE LADIES PLEASE COME TO ORDER

Comedy. 1 act. By Martha Norwood Gibson.

8 females. Interior.

At a meeting of the Center City Ladies' Cultural League the four officers' true thoughts reveal their inner selves, as they clash in a very ladylike way. The president is really rather stingy. The treasurer is beginning to look seedy. The secretary hates to wear her glasses. The vice-president can't keep her records straight. A typical club meeting with all the undercurrents brought out into the open for the audience to enjoy.

(Royalty, $5.00.)

Old-Fashioned Melodramas

(GAY NINETIES VARIETY)
(Budget Non-Royalty)

ONE-ACT

HE AIN'T DONE RIGHT BY NELL
3 male, 4 female

CURSE YOU, JACK DALTON
3 male, 4 female

DORA, THE BEAUTIFUL DISHWASHER
3 male, 4 female

EGAD, WHAT A CAD!
3 male, 4 female

FIREMAN SAVE MY CHILD
3 male, 5 female

GREAT WESTERN MELODRAMA
5 male, 2 female

HE DONE HER WRONG
2 male, 4 female

HER FATAL BEAUTY
3 male, 5 female

SHE WAS ONLY A FARMER'S DAUGHTER
3 male, 5 female

SOME DAY, PERHAPS
2 male, 2 female

GAY NINETIES SCRAPBOOK

GASLIGHT GAIETIES

(Variety Show)

Early Frost

by DOUGLAS PARKHIRST

Drama—1 Act

5 Female—Interior

A tender, yet gripping story of two sisters, Hannah and Louise, who live in a rambling, old house. Hannah has been considered peculiar ever since childhood, when a missing playmate was believed carried off by gypsies. When Alice, the sisters' little niece, comes to live with them, Hannah fearfully insists that she is the missing child returned. While playing in the attic, Alice is visited by a strange illusion, which almost leads her to solve the mystery of fifty years ago. Hannah, fearing her long-guarded secret will be discovered, tries to silence the little girl. It is this tense, cat-and-mouse game between the two that brings the play to a startling climax and affords the actors an opportunity for skillful playing, while holding the audience spellbound.

(Royalty, $5.00.)

An Overpraised Season

by RICHARD S. DUNLOP

A Play of Ideas—1 Act

4 male, 2 female—No setting required

A powerful and touching story, "An Overpraised Season" won six out of nine possible awards at the one-act contest in which it premiered. Numerous problems facing today's intelligent and sensitive adolescents are treated in the 40 minute play, which, in episode form, concerns two boys and a girl; a domineering, religiously fanatic mother; and a selfish, egocentric father. A narrator, somewhat like the Stage Manager of "Our Town," expounds the philosophy of the play. A quality play, "Season" is designed for advanced student performers.

(Royalty, $5.00.)

SO WONDERFUL (IN WHITE)
Drama. 1 act. By N. Richard Nusbaum.
9 females. Interior. Modern costumes. 25 minutes.

Margaret Shipman, a nurse in training, has brought to her calling bright hope and idealism. The test of this idealism comes when Shipman is confronted with the heartbreaks of her profession: The necessity to sacrifice a personal love, Charles; injustice as typified by the formalized rigidity and mercilessness of Miss Cresson, her superintendent; hypocrisy and meanness as exemplified by Eleanor De Witt; and tragedy in the suicide of Janey Held, a lonely narcotic addict. In the last moments of the play, when cause has piled upon effect and her idealism appears entirely in cloud and shadow, there emerges a new clarity, a maturer hope.
(Royalty, $5.00.)

SPY ME THIS ONE
Comedy. 1 act. By John Kirkpatrick.
7 females. Interior. Modern costumes. 35 minutes.

Twice before, when Evalina's husband went away on business, Evalina got into trouble. This time that charming lady takes up espionage work. With a secret service agent hiding behind a screen and the unfortunate maid locked up in a clothes-closet, Evalina prepares to receive a dangerous "spy." The "spy" no sooner arrives than in walks another, then another and still another. Evalina puts in a very busy evening!
(Royalty, $5.00.)

THE DEAR, DEAR CHILDREN
Comedy. 1 act. By Sophie Kerr.
8 females. Interior. Modern costumes. 30 minutes.

Mrs. Williard is having her troubles with her daughter, Esther, who would rather play tennis with her boy friend than help her mother get things ready for the visit of the library committee. Gradually the women arrive, each having a story to tell about how her children misbehave so violently that they wear her out. But at the height of the discussion a phone call is received, and we discover that a mutual friend of the ladies has given birth to a new baby. Immediately all the women begin to plan ways of congratulating the young mother on her extreme "good fortune."
(Royalty, $5.00.)

MIMI LIGHTS THE CANDLE

Drama. 1 act. By Edith Coulter.

1 male, 8 females. Interior. Modern costumes. 20 minutes.

One of the prize-winners in the General Federation of Women's Clubs Contest. A charming play about Christmas in which the age-old idea of the coming of the Christ Child is given an original and beautiful mode of treatment. The play can, however, be produced at any time of the year, since the story is universal.

(No Royalty.)

GUEST HOUSE, VERY EXCLUSIVE

Christmas play. 1 act. By Reby Edmond.

4 males, 6 females. Interior. Modern costumes. 30 minutes.

A Christmas play that is different. This is the story of a woman who longed for a family. She opens a very exclusive boarding house and attempts to weld the various individuals into one family. However, as Christmas Day dawns, they all have their own plans and she seems doomed to disappointment. What brings them together is a story in itself.

(Budget Play.)

THE CHRISTMAS APPLE

Christmas play. Adapted by Margaret D. Williams from the story by Ruth Sawyer.

6 males, 6 females, 2 interiors. Costumes, 18th Centi .y German. 30 minutes.

For generations the story has come down that if on Christmas Eve the perfect gift were presented to the Christ Chlid at the altar in the Cathedral, the Christ Child Himself would lean down and accept the gift from the giver. Silver and gold, jewels and embroidered silks are laid on the altar. Humbly old Herman walks up the aisle and presents the apple. Graciously the Christ Child accepts this gift of love, and lo! the miracle has come to pass.

(Budget Play.)

THE DESERT SHALL REJOICE
Play. 1 act. By Robert Finch.

7 males, 2 females. Modern costumes. 35 minutes.

On the Nevada desert highway is Nick's Place. On this night Nick confides to Dusty that he "hates Christmas." He refuses to allow any Christmas present here at Nick's Place. In spite of this, he finds time to overwhelm Dusty with kindness, to befriend two young travelers who are on their way to Bethlehem, Pennsylvania, and to give a present to his wife, which he insists is not a Christmas present. Made into the Academy Award picture, "Star in the Night."

(Royalty, $5.00.)

NO ROOM AT THE INN!
Christmas drama. 1 act. By Dorothy Yost.

17 males, 5 females (choir). Interior. Biblical costumes.
35 minutes.

The inn is crowded to overflow with people who have come to pay their taxes according to Herod's edict. The strange woman and her husband can find no accommodations and are forced to take shelter in the stable where her Child is born. Other travelers come, guided by the Star, including the Shepherds and the Magi and in the end all join worshiping the Christ Child.

(Royalty, $5.00.)

A KING SHALL REIGN!
Christmas play. 1 act. By Marion Wefer.

2 males, 4 females, extras. Interior. Biblical costumes.
20 minutes.

A Hebrew mother whose child was slain by Herod's soldiers is prostrate with grief. Others, tragically bereaved, try comforting her. Their talk touches upon Israel's promised King whose might and power of vengeance they long for. The mother rouses to listen and tell her vision of a King to whom she could give allegiance. She will not own one of blood and battle. Later, alone, she gives hospitality to travelers who flee the country with their child. As she puts grief aside to minister to them it is revealed that her King is born indeed and she has sheltered Him.

(Royalty, $5.00.)

A RAISIN IN THE SUN

By LORRAINE HANSBERRY

DRAMA

7 men, 3 women, 1 child—Interior

A Negro family is cramped in a flat on the south side of Chicago. They are a widow, her son (a chauffeur), his wife, his sister, and his little boy. The widow is expecting a $10,000 insurance settlement on her husband's death, and her son is constantly begging her to give him the money so that he can become co-owner of a liquor store. He wants to quit chauffeuring, to become a business man, and to be able to leave his son a little bit more than his own father, a bricklayer, had left him: this is the only way a Negro can continue to improve his lot. The widow, meantime, has placed a down-payment on a house where they can have sunlight, and be rid of roaches. The despair of the young husband is intense. His mother reluctantly turns over the remaining $6500 to him, as head of the house. He invests in the liquor store, his partner absconds, and his dream is forever dead. A representative from the better (white) neighborhood, into which they planned to move, calls on them and offers to reimburse them handsomely for their investment. But our young man now realizes that a little bit of dignity is all he can ever count on, and he plans to move his family to the new house.

(Royalty, $50-$25.)

PURLIE VICTORIOUS

By OSSIE DAVIS

COMEDY

6 men, 3 women—Exterior, 2 comp.

By taking all the cliches of plays, about the lovable old south and the love that existed between white masters and colored slaves, Ossie Davis has compounded a constantly comic play. Purlie Victorious has come back to his shabby cabin to announce that he will reacquire the local church and ring the freedom bell. There is an inheritance due to a colored cousin, which would be sufficient to buy the church, but unfortunately it also is controlled by the white-head plantation colonel. Purlie Victorious tries to send a newcomer to the colonel to impersonate the heiress, not only is she found out, but the colonel makes a pass at her. Eventually the church is recovered, services are again held in it, and the freedom bell rings. It is the dialogue, though, that makes the events so uproarious ("Are you trying to get non-violent with me, boy?") or human ("Oh, child, being colored can be a lot of fun when they ain't nobody looking"). There's uncommonly good sense in such a line as the one delivered to Purlie when he was about to beat the colonel with the colonel's well-worn bullwhip: "You can't do wrong just because it's right."

(Royalty, $50-$25.)

The Happy Hunter

(ALL GROUPS)
Comedy—CHARLES FEYDEAU

English Adaptation by Barnett Shaw
7 Men, 3 Women—2 Interiors

Chandel tells Yvonne he is going hunting with Castillo, but when Castillo turns up unexpectedly, she sees the hoax, and therefore decides to yield to Roussel's amorous advances, going to his bachelor den with him. But, across the hall, Chandel is having a rendezvous with Madame Castillo. A hectic evening ensues, complicated by an eccentric landlady and by the appearance of Yvonne's nephew, whose girl friend used to live there. The police, seeking Madame Castillo's lover, grab Roussel, while Chandel escapes through the window and runs off with Roussel's trousers. The mix-up unravels in act three, with one surprise after the other, Yvonne winning all tricks while her husband gets the punishment.

ROYALTY, $35-$25

A Gown for His Mistress

(Little Theatre) Farce
GEORGE FEYDEAU

English Translation by Barnett Shaw
4 Men, 6 Females—Interior
Can be played 1900 Period or Chic Modern

A wild and saucy matrimonial mix-up by the celebrated author of A FLEA IN HER EAR.

Dr. Moulineaux stays out all night after a futile attempt to meet his mistress, Suzanne, at the Opera Ball. He tells his wife he has been up all night with a friend, Bassinet, who is near death, but at that moment Bassinet walks in. Upbraided by his mother-in-law for his infidelity, he decides he must no longer allow Suzanne to pretend to be a patient. For a hide-away, he rents an apartment that formerly belonged to a dressmaker. In Act II he is courting Suzanne in his new apartment when her husband walks in. Posing as a dressmaker he gets rid of the husband momentarily, but is caught in a desperate entanglement when his wife, his mother-in-law, Bassinet, and Bassinet's wife appear. In Act III, Moulineaux's household is in an uproar but he manages to lie his way out of it all with the help of Bassinet who has a photograph that seems to solve everything. Outstanding male and female roles. The play moves rapidly and is an excellent work-out for alert actors and actresses.

ROYALTY, $35-$25

#12